COPING IN A CHANGING WORLD

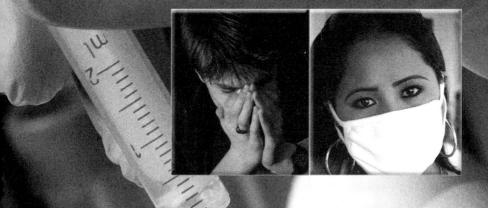

Avian Flu

Tamra Orr

ROSEN
PUBLISHING®

New York

As always, to my family, who puts up with listening to me tell them everything I've learned when researching a book

Published in 2007 by The Roscn Publishing Group, Inc.
29 East 21st Street, New York, NY 10010

First Edition

Library of Congress Cataloging-in-Publication Data

Orr, Tamra.
Avian flu / Tamra Orr.—1st ed.
    p. cm.—(Coping in a changing world)
Includes bibliographical references and index.
ISBN-13: 978-1-4042-0950-3
ISBN-10: 1-4042-0950-6 (library binding)
1. Avian influenza—Juvenile literature. I. Title.
RA644.I6O77 2007
614.5'18—dc22

                                                              2006019286

Manufactured in the United States of America

Contents

CHAPTER ONE

Avian Flu: Countering Fear with Facts

ALL IN ALL, THERE IS NO REASON TO PANIC. AT THIS POINT, YOU HAVE LITTLE CHANCE OF CONTRACTING AVIAN FLU, ESPECIALLY IF YOU DO NOT HANDLE BIRDS OR COME INTO CONTACT WITH UNCOOKED POULTRY VERY OFTEN.

N ews reports repeatedly trumpet the same alarming "facts": that avian flu is spreading across the globe, killing thousands in a deadly pandemic. However, the truth is considerably less alarming.

"Avian flu" generally refers to infection in birds by the type A (H5N1) influenza virus (although when humans are infected by this virus, they, too, are described as having been infected with avian flu). Type A is a broad category of flu viruses that can infect humans and lead to pandemics. The "H" and the "N" in bird flu's official name refer to two proteins that reside on the outside of the virus and allow it to penetrate a cell and, after reproducing itself, exit the cell in order to move on and infect other cells.

Wild birds are often infected by the A (H5N1) virus. Though it resides in their intestines, they rarely get sick from it. However, they can pass the virus on to domesticated birds such as chickens, turkeys, and ducks. These birds are much more vulnerable to the virus and often get sick and die when infected. More severe strains of the virus can result in a 90 to 100 percent mortality rate in poultry.

It is true that avian flu has spread to humans, and the number of human cases has increased over the last several years since the first documented one in 1997. Yet it is also true that, given the number of birds that have the virus, the number of humans who become infected is low.

At this point, it is extremely rare for the avian flu to be passed from person to person. Furthermore, there has never been a documented case of person-to-person-to-person transmission, meaning the virus does not seem to continue on to a third person after the second person is infected. Because of these factors, the possibility of widespread infection is greatly reduced. Yet scientists fear the virus may mutate in such a way that person-to-person transmission will become easier, leading to the possibility of a devastating pandemic. Preparations are being made for this worst-case scenario.

All in all, there is no reason to panic. You have little chance of contracting avian flu, especially if you do not handle birds or come into contact with uncooked poultry very often. Even if the virus mutates and begins to spread from human to human, epidemiologists and lab researchers are working overtime to test effective antiviral medications and develop a vaccine that will prevent infection in the first place. Keep in mind that very few flu scares have emerged as the deadly scourge they were initially feared to be.

One infamous flu did indeed wreak death and destruction worldwide—the 1918 Spanish flu—and it is the communal, historical memory of this killer that has many people fearful now. Yet our twenty-first-century world is in a much better position to stave off catastrophe and protect itself from the ravages of infectious disease.

TEN FACTS ABOUT AVIAN FLU

1. Avian flu is found in wild and domesticated birds. It has appeared in other animals after they ate raw chicken.

2. The only human cases of avian flu so far have been the result of people who have been in direct contact with contaminated birds.
3. It is not easy for humans to become infected with avian flu. Even people who have handled infected birds often do not become infected.
4. The standard flu shot will not protect against the H5N1 virus. An effective avian flu vaccine has not yet been manufactured.
5. President Bush is dedicating billions in federal funds to ready the nation for a potential pandemic.
6. To date, there have been millions of birds killed that either had the virus or were suspected of having it.
7. As of August 2006, there have been more than 200 reported cases of avian flu in people. So far, 139 of these people have died.
8. Pandemics often come in waves, spaced weeks to months apart.
9. Three of the main ways that avian flu could reach the United States is through migrating birds, exotic bird trades, and cockfighting.
10. In humans, the avian flu primarily attacks the lungs, affecting their ability to breathe.

Chapter Two

The Spanish Flu of 1918

SCHOOLS AND CHURCHES WERE SHUT DOWN. BUSINESSES AND LIBRARIES CLOSED. PUBLIC GATHERINGS WERE CANCELED . . . TENS OF THOUSANDS OF PEOPLE DIED IN EVERY MAJOR CITY AROUND THE WORLD.

I t snuck in quietly when no one was looking. Everyone was far too busy paying close attention to reports about the war—the war that was supposed to end all wars. It was 1918, and America was immersed in fighting World War I, as were many of the world's nations. Americans were consumed with casualty lists, battle details, and news from the front lines. Communications came primarily through telegraph, as telephone service was still too new and unreliable. Travel was by steamship or train. Women were still fighting for the right to vote. Mercifully, then as today, baseball provided a welcome distraction from the cares of the day. Babe Ruth, not yet a New York Yankee, had just led the Boston Red Sox to victory in the World Series.

Sometime in the fall of 1918, however, a new threat silently emerged. It was not a hostile country, a new type of destructive and deadly weapon, or even a natural disaster. This one respected no national boundaries, cared nothing about what side of the world war its victims were on, and knew nothing of mercy. It was a monstrous, indifferent enemy that no one expected and very few would escape.

The Spanish Lady had come to town.

ATTACK FROM WITHIN

At the end of 1918, an article in the *Journal of the American Medical Association* summed up this time period the best. It said, "1918 has gone: a year momentous as the termination of the most cruel war in the annals of the human race; a year which marked the end, at least for a time, of man's destruction of man; unfortunately a year in which developed a most fatal infectious disease causing the death of hundreds of thousands of human beings. Medical science for four and one half years devoted itself to putting men on the firing line and keeping them there. Now it must turn with its whole might to combating the greatest enemy of all: infectious disease."[1]

It all began on a spring day at Fort Riley, Kansas. This huge military camp sprawled over 20,000 acres, was home to 26,000 soldiers, and included stables for thousands of horses and mules. The men here were tough. Not only did they know what it was like to fight in a savage war, but they also had endured a prairie climate that brought them blisteringly hot summers, bitterly frigid winters, and blinding dust storms. On this day, just like many others, there was a putrid stench in the air from the burning of the nine tons of manure the animals produced each week. The wind blew the pungent smell from one end of the camp to another.

When company cook Albert Gitchell reported to the infirmary with what he called a "bad cold," the medical staff took little note of it. Minutes later, Corporal Lee W. Drake followed with a similar ailment. This was regarded as a simple coincidence. By noon, 100 men had shown up at the infirmary complaining of sore throats and fevers. This was more than a little unusual and clearly no coincidence. By the end of the week, there were 500 men in the infirmary. Something was terribly wrong at Fort Riley.

These men were young and in their prime. One minute they would be out on maneuvers, the next they were complaining of a fever and deep cough. Breathing soon became impossible. Their lungs shut down. Their faces turned blue. Soldiers died before doctors even determined what was wrong with them. Bulletins about this strange new flu were sent out, but these warnings were initially downplayed in the media. Radio stations carefully censored what was read over the air. They did not want to say anything negative that could possibly hurt the morale of the soldiers or create panic in the general population.

The problem not only persisted, however—it spread. Soon, other military camps around the world were being hit by this baffling illness. When Spain's King Alphonse III fell victim to it, too, his condition was carefully followed in the newspapers. Unlike other countries, Spain was not involved enough in the war to censor what was considered to be troubling news. Since it was the first nation to announce officially the presence of this new disease, it quickly became known as the "Spanish Lady."

The 1918 influenza pandemic was called a number of different names. These included:

- The Spanish Lady
- La Grippe
- Spanish flu
- The Naples Soldier

CAMP DEVENS

In August 1918, a large group of soldiers stationed at Camp Devens, near Boston, Massachusetts, became ill, and many died. They had the same symptoms as the Fort Riley soldiers. Medical doctors were completely confounded by this new disease. In recent years, there had been many medical victories over such formerly lethal diseases as smallpox, anthrax, rabies, diphtheria, and meningitis. It seemed impossible that physicians could not figure this one out, too.

Victor Vaughan, former president of the American Medical Association, was ordered to go to Camp Devens and observe the symptoms and disease progression in the men there. What he saw changed his life and his attitude toward medicine forever:

> The saddest part of my life was when I witnessed the hundreds of deaths of the soldiers in the Army camps and did not know what to do. I saw hundreds of young stalwart men in uniform coming into the wards of the hospital. Every bed was full, yet others crowded in. Their faces wore a bluish

cast; a cough brought up blood-stained sputum. This infection, like war, kills the young, vigorous, robust adults . . . The husky male either made a speedy and rather abrupt recovery or was likely to die. At that moment I decided never again to prate about the great achievements of medical science and to humbly admit our dense ignorance in this case.[2]

The same day this letter was written, sixty-three soldiers died while Vaughn could do nothing more than watch it happen.

Meanwhile, Rupert Blue, the Surgeon General of the United States Public Health Services, was desperately trying to round up more doctors to examine the hundreds of ill patients throughout the nation's military camps. There were precious few doctors to call on. Most were already busy fighting in the war. Blue, despite criticism for doing so, called on retired doctors, disabled doctors, anyone he could possibly find. Eventually, he gathered 250 physicians. This was a big help—but it wasn't enough. These doctors were about to do battle with a virus-based illness. And in 1918, there was no clear agreement on what a virus or influenza was, let alone how to treat it.

This strange illness was also affecting the overall progress of the war. On both sides, attacks were either postponed or cancelled because there were not enough healthy men to go out and wage battle. By early summer, the Spanish Lady had traveled far beyond the United States and western Europe to Russia, North Africa, India, China, Japan, and New Zealand. It had killed tens of thousands of people. Then, just as mysteriously as the flu appeared, it disappeared at summer's end.

People believed the worst was over. They heaved a collective sigh of relief. Sadly, they were wrong. A second wave of killing flu was on its way.

SECOND TIME AROUND

In the fall, the Spanish Lady returned with a vengeance. In Boston alone, there were more than 200 deaths a day. In New York City, 851 people died in one day, 700 times the usual death rate. The Department of Health had no choice but to issue a public warning that an epidemic was underway. Life changed in homes all over the world. Schools and churches were shut down. Businesses and libraries closed. Public gatherings were canceled. In houses in which children lived, passersby could hear young voices singing a new song that was all the more haunting for its brave attempt at dark humor:

> I had a little bird
> Its name was Enza.
> I opened up the window
> And in-flu-enza.

At last, not knowing what else to do, Congress gave the United States Public Health Services $1 million to figure out what the Spanish flu actually was—and how to stop it in its tracks.

The Spanish flu was so deadly and fast-moving that it actually began to raise suspicions in people. Could the Germans be behind this somehow? Was this sabotage or germ warfare? Could spies have seeded the military camps with some kind of powerful new virus? These fears were not soothed by a statement from Lieutenant Colonel Philip Doane, head of the Health and Sanitation section of the Emergency Fleet Corporation: "It would be quite easy for one of these German agents to turn loose influenza germs in a theatre or some other place where large numbers of persons are assembled," he said. "The Germans have started epidemics in Europe and there is no reason why they should be particularly gentle with America."[3]

Other theories circulated, too. Some people believed that toxic gases emitted by dead soldiers and exploding munitions had mixed and become a poisonous vapor. When the flu eventually spread beyond the military camps into the general population, that theory was proven false. Other possible explanations included everything from air stagnation, coal dust, or fleas, to "distemper" in cats and dogs or dirty dishwater.

Public life in large cities like New York became increasingly strange. Coughing and sneezing were legally banned and carried stiff fines if ignored. If people ventured out, most wore face masks. Doctors, at a loss on how to treat the patients who overflowed their waiting rooms, recommended anything they could think of such as quinine tablets (used to treat fevers and malaria), bleeding, castor oil (which purges the body of waste), morphine (a painkiller), enemas (which cleanse the colon and intestines), aspirin, tobacco, hot baths, cold baths, and iron tonics. Traditional folk remedies were suggested for flu prevention, including putting salt up the nose, chewing garlic gum, or eating only onions. Although these practices never actually worked, at least they made people feel as if they were doing something to protect themselves from this phantom enemy.

Tens of thousands of people died in every major city around the world. Patients overflowed the hospitals and spilled out into the streets. Emergency care was established in parks and playgrounds. The only continent not affected by this powerful flu was Antarctica. Some remote and insular populations like the Inuit in the Arctic Circle—who had little previous exposure to the diseases of the developed world and therefore less immunity—were nearly destroyed by the pandemic. Coffins were in such short supply that they had to be protected by armed guards or else people would steal them.

TRYING TO FORGET

As 1918 began to wind down, the long world war in Europe finally came to an end. At the same time, the flu also began to lessen its terrifying grip around the globe. Ever so slowly, the number of people dying began to drop. When statistics were tallied, more American soldiers (57,000) were killed by the flu than in the world war (53,500) that was coming to an end. Millions of people from every corner of the world had died. The majority of them had been between twenty and thirty-four years old. Estimates of the number of fatalities worldwide ranged widely, between 20 million and 100 million.

Amazingly, information about one of the more catastrophic events in world history is not always found in modern school textbooks. Somehow, this vicious killer not only ripped its way across the planet, it also managed to avoid the lasting attention of historians and the media. People simply did not want to discuss such a black period in time, marked by violent war and deadly disease. Instead, they wanted to celebrate the return of peace and focus on life returning to something like normal again. Magazines, newspapers, and radio no longer reported on the Spanish Lady. It was shoved aside as a topic too bleak to discuss.

This avoidance of the subject was so effective that even today schoolchildren rarely learn about the 1918 flu pandemic. It has only been recent events in history (such as the Hong Kong flu and the Avian flu) that have made people look back on that year and examine how the world endured the outbreak. The Spanish flu is now being studied for what survival lessons it might have for future generations experiencing pandemics of new and mysterious diseases.

Now, close to a century later, researchers have studied the preserved remains of some of the victims of the 1918 flu pandemic. They wanted to try and find out just why this particular virus killed so many so fast. It did not take long for them to determine why it had been so devastating: it was a type of virus that humans had never encountered before, so they had absolutely no immunity to it. They also discovered the source: it was an A type virus—the most fatal one of all—that first occurred in birds and mutated in such a way that it could leap to humans and infect them.

A LETTER FROM THE FRONT

Dr. Roy Grist, a military physician, wrote this letter back home from Camp Devens, in Massachusetts. It was discovered in a trunk in 1959 and donated to the Department of Epidemiology at the University of Michigan. It offers a personal insight into the terror of the Spanish Lady.

Camp Devens, Mass.
Surgical Ward No. 16
29 September 1918

My dear Burt,

Camp Devens is near Boston and has about 50,000 men, or did have before this epidemic broke loose. It also has the base hospital for the Division of the Northeast. This epidemic started about four weeks ago and has developed so rapidly that the camp is demoralized and all ordinary work is held up 'til it has passed. All assemblages of soldiers taboo. These men start with what appears to be an attack of la grippe or influenza, and when brought to the hospital they very rapidly develop the most vicious type of pneumonia that has ever been seen. Two hours after admission they have the mahogany spots over the cheekbones, and a few hours later you can begin to see the cyanosis [bluish or purplish discoloration] extending from their ears and spreading all over the face, until it is hard to distinguish the colored men from the white. It is only a matter of a few hours then until death comes, and it is simply a struggle for air until they suffocate. It is horrible. One can stand to see one, two, or twenty men die, but to see these poor devils dropping like flies sort of gets on your nerves. We have been averaging about 100 deaths per day, and still keeping it up. There is no doubt in my mind that there is a new mixed infection here, but what I don't know. My total time is taken up hunting rales [rattling sounds in the chest], rales dry or moist, sibilant [hissing or whistling] or crepitant [crackling] or any other of the hundred things that one may find in the chest, they all mean but one thing here—pneumonia—and that means in about all cases death.

The normal number of doctors here is about 25 and that has been increased to over 250, all of whom (of course excepting me) have temporary orders—"Return to your proper station on completion of work"—Mine says, "Permanent Duty," but I have been in the Army just long enough to learn that it doesn't always mean what it says. So I don't know what will happen to me at the end of this. We have lost an outrageous number of nurses and doctors, and the little town of Ayer is a sight. It takes special trains to carry away the dead. For several days there were no coffins and the bodies piled up something fierce, we used to go down to the morgue (which is just back of my ward) and look at the boys laid out in long rows. It beats any sight they ever had in France after a battle. An extra long barracks has been vacated for the use of the morgue, and it would make any man sit up and take notice to walk down the long lines of dead soldiers all dressed up and laid out in double rows. We have no relief here; you get up in the morning at 5:30 and work steady till about 9:30 p.m., sleep, then go at it again. Some of the men of course have been here all the time, and they are tired.

If this letter seems somewhat disconnected overlook it, for I have been called away from it a dozen times, the last time just now by the Office ["Officer"?] of the Day, who came in to tell me that they have not as yet found at any of the autopsies any case beyond the red hepatitis stage. It kills them before it gets that far.

Good-by old Pal.
"God be with you till we meet again" . . .
Roy[4]

CHAPTER THREE

Other Pandemics Throughout History

THE BOTTOM LINE WITH PANDEMICS:
AS MUCH AS WE WISH WE COULD,
WE SIMPLY CAN'T PREDICT THEM
WITH ANY ACCURACY . . . IT CAN BE
RIGHT ON TOP OF YOU—OR IT CAN
PASS YOU RIGHT BY.

P andemics are nothing new to our world. Reports of them date back as far as 430 BC. They always wear different masks, of course. Some came in the form of typhoid and plague, others as smallpox and cholera. Influenza pandemics, however, were not first recorded until 1889. By taking the time to study each one of history's pandemics carefully, today's experts can learn vital lessons about how to prepare for the next one. That there will be a next one is considered inevitable by almost everyone in the field. The only real questions are when, and how deadly and difficult to contain and combat it will be.

PANDEMIC: A WORLDWIDE OUTBREAK OF INFLUENZA

From an October 17, 2005, Centers for Disease Control and Prevention (CDC) report:

> An influenza pandemic is a global outbreak of disease that occurs when a new influenza A virus appears or "emerges" in the human population, causes serious illness, and then spreads easily from person to person worldwide. Pandemics are different from seasonal outbreaks or "epidemics" of influenza. Seasonal outbreaks are caused by subtypes of influenza viruses that already circulate among people, whereas pandemic outbreaks are caused by new subtypes, by

subtypes that have never circulated among people, or by subtypes that have not circulated among people for a long time. Past influenza pandemics have led to high levels of illness, death, social disruptions, and economic loss.

THE ASIAN FLU

In the late 1950s, the influenza virus A (H2N2)—known as the Asian flu—was sweeping the world. By the time it ended, it had caused approximately 70,000 deaths in the United States and two million worldwide. It was first identified in northern China early in 1957, and it reached the United States during the summer of that year. The first wave hit small children, young adults, and pregnant women the hardest. The second wave, which appeared three months later, primarily targeted the elderly. A vaccine was hastily manufactured and given out, often for free. Two injections were necessary, no less than three weeks apart.

THE HONG KONG FLU

Just about a decade later, a new flu emerged and began spreading across the world. In 1968, the A (H3N2) virus first appeared in Hong Kong and, in a matter of months, reached the United States. Schools, churches, and offices were empty. On New York City's Broadway, plays were either cancelled or understudies were called in to replace ailing stars. The Los Angeles Rams football team had to stop practicing because so many of the players were ill. Deaths peaked over the holiday season, preying mainly on people over the age of sixty-five. Vaccines began shipping in mid-November. By the time the pandemic was brought under control, the Hong Kong flu had caused roughly 34,000 U.S. deaths and one million worldwide.

THE SWINE FLU

In a now hauntingly familiar scenario, the swine flu began when a nineteen-year-old private named David Lewis from Massachusetts fell to the ground and died after a march at Fort Dix in New Jersey. He had already told his drill sergeant that he felt weak and tired, but he went on the march anyway. Twenty-four hours later, Lewis was dead. It was February 5, 1976.

When four other soldiers got sick, health officials got scared. They knew exactly what had happened at Fort Riley in 1918 and vowed that there would be no repeat of that epic tragedy. There were alarming similarities, however. Secretary of Health F. David Matthews stated, "There is evidence there will be a major flu epidemic this coming fall. The indication is that we will see a return of the 1918 flu virus that is the most virulent form of flu. In 1918, half a million people died. The projections are that this virus will kill one million Americans in 1976."[1]

Doctors from the CDC, as well as prominent medical personnel such as Jonas Salk and Albert Sabin, inventors of the polio vaccine, arranged an emergency meeting in Washington, D.C., to discuss how to respond to what they saw as a potential pandemic waiting to explode. Finally, they came to the conclusion that mass inoculation of the public was necessary. They went to President Gerald Ford and asked for $135 million to inoculate every man, woman, and child in the United States.

On August 12, 1976, Congress approved the funds requested to fight swine flu, so called because it stemmed from a virus that is found naturally in pigs. The government formed the National Influenza Immunization Program. Dr. W. Delano Meriwether of the Department of Health, Education, and Welfare was given the daunting job of finding a way to vaccinate 220 million Americans in less than five months. It was not easy. To make things more complicated, there was an unexpected problem. Since this vaccination would be made quite rapidly, the manufacturers refused to be held responsible for any negative reactions or side effects it might have. The doctors administering it also refused to be held responsible for mishaps. Even the nation's insurance companies wanted nothing to do with insuring the program against accidental illness or death. In the end, the government had no choice but to state that it would be held accountable for any problems that might occur. Little did the nation's leaders know that they would come to deeply regret that promise.

When doctors and nurses began immunizing against swine flu in October, they administered one million shots in the first week. Two weeks later, it was up to four million. Within a month, it was up to six million. By mid-December, forty million people had been vaccinated. Then, at the height of the immunization process, doctors' worst fears began to be realized.

Almost a dozen different states began to report an apparently dangerous side effect from the swine flu shot. In some patients, it appeared to cause a serious neurological disorder called Guillain-Barre syndrome, which causes muscular weakness, especially in the hands and feet. By January 1977, there were more than 500 cases reported, including 25 deaths. The vaccination program was stopped immediately. By the end of the year, more than 1,098 cases of Guillain-Barre had been diagnosed, resulting in millions of dollars in lawsuits against the only responsible party—the U.S. government. What had started out as an emergency effort to protect people had turned into an expensive catastrophe. To add insult to injury, the predicted swine flu pandemic never arrived. The vaccinations had not been necessary after all, but they had created hundreds of Guillain-Barre victims.

In the book *Bird Flu: Everything You Need to Know about the Next Pandemic,* Marc Siegel writes, "Swine flu showed not only that you can rush to judgment, wasting time and money ramping up for a worst-case scenario that never comes, but that in doing so, there may be significant costs to people's health."[2] This is a valuable cautionary lesson in today's climate of near-panic and media hysteria over a predicted avian flu pandemic.

A PANDEMIC TIMELINE

430 BC In Greece, typhoid fever kills a quarter of Athenian troops and a quarter of the general population within four years.

AD 165–180 In the Mediterranean area, Antonine plague, most likely a form of smallpox, kills a quarter of those infected and five million in all. During a second outbreak from 251 to 266, during its peak, 5,000 people are reported dying in Rome every day.

541 Plague of Justinian, first recorded outbreak of the bubonic plague. Records indicate that at its height, 10,000 a day are dying and up to a quarter of the population of the eastern Mediterranean is killed.

1300s The Black Death (bubonic plague) begins in Europe. Twenty million Europeans die in six years, a quarter of the total population.

1816 The first cholera pandemic begins in India. It is followed by additional cholera pandemics in 1829–1851, 1852–1860, 1863–1875, 1866, 1899–1923, and 1961–1966.

INFLUENZA PANDEMICS

1889–1890 Asiatic flu

1918 Spanish flu kills between 20 million and 100 million people worldwide.

1957 Asian flu kills two million worldwide.

1968 Hong Kong flu kills one million worldwide.

NEAR PANDEMICS

1976 Swine flu
1999 West Nile virus
2003 Sudden acute respiratory syndrome (SARS)

NEAR PANDEMICS

In addition to the certified pandemics discussed above, there have been several other close calls with diseases that threatened to rage out of control but thankfully didn't. They generated headlines, frightened the public, and placed physicians and hospitals on high alert. Yet they turned out to be far less severe than suspected, proving that forecasting the extent and progression of a pandemic is a complicated science that even the most knowledgeable researchers struggle with and often fail at. Tracking the progress of these illnesses, however, helps to demonstrate how frighteningly fast they can spread and document how they behave.

West Nile Virus

In 1999, before the current concern over avian flu, the world was becoming increasingly uneasy over the threat of an epidemic of the so-called West Nile virus. The carriers of this virus were mosquitoes that, in turn, had been infected by the birds they landed on and fed on. The first indication of the virus's presence in any given area was the sudden appearance of dead birds that did not seem to have been shot by humans or killed by animal predators. It was not long before it became clear that mosquitoes were carrying the virus, too. Because mosquitoes are only active at certain times of the year, this virus is considered a seasonal epidemic.

The severity of West Nile virus symptoms depends on the individual. About 80 percent of people who are infected will not show any symptoms at all. Approximately 20 percent will display symptoms, which include:

- Fever
- Headache
- Body aches
- Neck stiffness
- Numbness
- Nausea
- Vomiting
- Swollen lymph glands
- Skin rash on chest, stomach, and back

About 1 in 150 people who are infected with West Nile virus, however, will develop far more serious problems. These can include:

- High fever
- Stupor
- Disorientation
- Coma
- Tremors
- Convulsions
- Muscle weakness

- Vision loss
- Paralysis

According to the CDC, the West Nile virus's growth and spread from year to year have begun to slow. Although there were 9,175 cases and 230 deaths in 2003, the 2005 record reported only 2,949 cases with 116 deaths. It has not affected enough people in enough places to qualify as the pandemic some feared it might become.

While there is no treatment for West Nile virus, the drop in new cases and fatalities is attributed to anti-mosquito spraying by municipalities and people being aware of the risk factors of getting bitten by mosquitoes and taking steps to lessen that risk, like staying indoors at dawn and dusk, wearing long-sleeved shirts and long pants, and spraying themselves and their clothing with insect repellent.

SARS

Beginning in late 2002, hundreds of people in China's Guangdong Province began turning up in hospitals with a mysterious respiratory illness. Symptoms included headache, high fever, chills, an overall feeling of discomfort, and body aches. Later, a cough developed and usually pneumonia as well. A handful of victims died.

In February 2003, a man later referred to by epidemiologists as Patient A traveled from Guangdong Province to visit his family in Hong Kong. Soon after he arrived he checked into a hospital, but not before infecting a dozen people at his hotel. In their subsequent travels, these twelve, in turn, spread the illness to Hong Kong, Vietnam, Singapore, Ireland, Germany, and Canada.

Patient A died the day after checking into the hospital. By then, two of his family members and four hospital workers were also sick. An officer of the World Health Organization (WHO), Dr. Carlo Urbani, named the condition SARS, which stands for sudden acute respiratory syndrome.

Days later, a seventy-eight-year-old woman who had visited Hong Kong died in Toronto, Canada. Meanwhile, in Hong Kong, ninety-nine cases of this new and very deadly illness appeared, mostly in health-care workers. All were connected to a patient who had stayed at the same hotel as Patient A. By mid-March, the WHO issued a global SARS alert warning travelers who had been in Asia to watch for possible symptoms.

Soon after, eleven cases of SARS were reported in Canada. In Singapore and Hong Kong, thousands of people were put into quarantine, and schools were closed. At that point, more than 1,400 people world-wide had contracted SARS, with fifty-three fatalities. Among the dead was Dr. Urbani of the WHO. By early April, WHO reported 2,353 cases—84 of them fatal—in sixteen countries. A week later, the number of infections climbed to 2,671.

Researchers who had been working furiously to identify and understand the new disease finally made some important discoveries. They determined that SARS was caused by a coronavirus, the same family of viruses that causes the common cold. At the end of the month, the number of infections was up to 5,000, with 321 fatalities. Travel advisories were posted warning people not to fly to some of the most seriously affected countries.

At last, in July 2003, WHO officials announced that SARS was finally under control, and all travel advisories were lifted. More than 8,000 people had been infected in thirty-two countries, and 744 patients had died. The SARS outbreak was not extensive or prolonged enough to qualify as an epidemic or a pandemic, but it was sudden and deadly enough to frighten people and get the attention of health organizations around the world. Sadly, it was also enough to severely damage the Asian economy. The specter of infectious disease shut down much of the region's daily business and greatly harmed its tourist industry. It is estimated that $30 billion in revenue was lost before the SARS scare was over.

Epidemics and pandemics have been a part of world history for centuries. They can be identified, tracked, and studied. However, the one thing they cannot be is predicted. Sometimes, they can look like they are coming straight at us—remember ebola, mad cow disease, and hantavirus?—and then miss by a mile. Other times, they really do arrive whether they were anticipated or not. As Dr. Jeffrey Green writes in his book *The Bird Flu Pandemic: Can It Happen? Will It Happen?*, "The bottom line with pandemics: As much as we wish we could, we simply can't predict them with any accuracy. They're like trains rolling down the tracks. You can hear the rumbling, but you don't always know which way it's going. It can be right on top of you—or it can pass you right by."[3]

CHAPTER FOUR

The Nuts and Bolts of Viruses and Pandemics

COMPARING A VIRUS TO A BACTERIA IS TANTAMOUNT TO COMPARING A BOOMERANG TO A SNAKE. ONE IS INANIMATE. THE OTHER IS ALIVE. BOTH, OF COURSE, CAN KILL YOU IF YOU HAPPEN TO GET IN THEIR WAY.

T o truly understand the extent and gravity of a potential pandemic like avian flu, you first must have a basic understanding of biology. Let's take a look at how a virus works.

All types of influenza are caused by viruses. Viruses are also what cause other illnesses such as AIDS, hepatitis, and Ebola. Viruses are very tiny, about one-millionth of an inch long. Millions of them can fit on the head of a pin. They are usually shaped like rods or spheres and are hollow. They have been called the "ultimate parasites" and "masters of interspecies navigation" for their ability to pass from one kind of creature to another and use their host for nourishment and reproduction.

Viruses are not the same thing as bacteria. A virus is essentially dead, while bacteria are alive. In addition, viruses are single cells and cannot reproduce on their own. They have to invade the cells of a host in order to replicate. "Comparing a virus to a bacteria," explains Dr. Jeffrey Greene, "is tantamount to comparing a boomerang to a snake. One is inanimate. The other is alive. Both, of course, can kill you if you happen to get in their way."[1]

THE JOB OF A VIRUS

A virus particle (a virion) is made up of three things: nucleic acid, which contain the virus's genetic instructions; a protein, which protects the virus; and a membrane that surrounds the protein. Viruses basically have only two jobs in life. First, they are designed to invade their hosts with a vengeance. Without a host, they simply cannot function. So they just lie about, waiting for the perfect host to come along. Once they spot it, they force their way in, through the host's nose, mouth, or broken skin.

Having gained access to a host, viruses next target what cells they want to attack, bind themselves to those cells, force their way in, and then inject their poison. This poison convinces the cell's enzymes to make parts for more virus particles. These particles gather together to form new viruses, which then break free from the host cell, often destroying it in the process. They then move on to infect other healthy cells and repeat the process, until the host is besieged by disease.

The second main job of a virus is to mutate. Each time viruses mutate, their ability to infect a host changes, too. They go in, grab genes of other viruses already present in the host, and alter their own genetic code in the process. This gives them new tools with which to penetrate and infect a host. The mutations can help the virus survive standard treatments and attack the host with new strength. Mutations also help viruses "leap" from animal to human populations. Sometimes, the leap is direct, as with hantavirus (a rodent-to-human virus) and monkey pox. Other times, it has to go through a liaison, like mosquitoes (such as West Nile virus, which moves from birds to mosquitoes to humans).

TYPE A FLU VIRUSES

All influenza viruses are divided into three types, depending on their structure. They are called A, B, and C. While B and C affect humans only, A can infect both animals and people. B and C are also considered rather mild, while type A is the lethal kind that causes pandemics such as the Spanish flu.

Type A viruses are further divided into two subtypes: fifteen strains of hemagglutinin (HA) and nine strains of neuraminidase (NA). These strains are all constantly evolving through two different processes: antigenic drift (small, permanent, ongoing changes in the genetic material) and antigenic shift (sudden, major changes in the genetic material).

Avian flu is a type A virus, and as such it is extremely dangerous. It can mutate directly or indirectly into a human flu, and that is what has health organizations like the CDC and WHO nervous. In 1918, a bird flu mutated into a human flu and wreaked havoc throughout the world. The question is—is it about to happen again?

CONDITIONS REQUIRED FOR A PANDEMIC TO OCCUR

1. A virus capable of infecting humans establishes a global presence in the animal world.
2. There must be a new flu virus subtype to which the human population has no immunity.
3. The new virus infects people, and they get seriously ill.
4. The virus is easily spread from person to person.

The way that a virus spreads depends on what type it is. The most common methods are:

- Carrier organisms (mosquitoes, birds, etc.)
- The air
- Direct transfer of body fluids from one person to another (saliva, sweat, nasal secretions, blood, etc.)
- Surfaces on which these body fluids have been

PANDEMIC STAGES

Episodes of pandemic are seen as consisting of six distinct phases and three periods of progression. Avian flu is currently considered to be in phase 3.

Interpandemic Period

Phase 1 No new influenza virus subtypes have been detected in humans. An influenza virus subtype that has caused human infection may be present in animals. If present in animals, the risk of human infection or disease is considered to be low.

Phase 2 No new influenza virus subtypes have been detected in humans. However, a circulating animal influenza virus subtype poses a substantial risk of human disease.

Pandemic Alert Period

Phase 3 Human infection(s) with a new subtype, but no human-to-human spread or, at least, rare instances of spread to a close contact.

Phase 4 Small cluster(s) with limited human-to-human transmission but spread is highly localized, suggesting that the virus is not well adapted to humans.

Phase 5 Small cluster(s) with limited human-to-human spread, still localized, suggesting that the virus is becoming increasingly better adapted to humans but may not yet be fully transmissible (substantial pandemic risk).

Pandemic Period

Phase 6 Pandemic: increased and sustained transmission in general population.[2]

Viruses can destroy creatures millions of times larger than they are in a very brief period of time. In a typical year, approximately 36,000 people die of the standard seasonal flu that goes around every winter. Because avian flu is still so alien and unfamiliar an invader of the human body, our immune systems have no tools whatsoever to fight it effectively. As Dr. David Nabarro, chief avian flu coordinator for the United Nations, puts it, "We spend billions to protect ourselves from threats that may not exist, from missiles, bombs, and human combatants, but pathogens from the animal kingdom are something against which we are appallingly badly protected, and our investment in pandemic insurance is minute."[3]

CHAPTER FIVE

The Emergence of Avian Flu

HOSPITALS WOULD BE COMPLETELY OVERWHELMED, BUSINESSES WOULD GO BANKRUPT . . . AND THERE WOULD PROBABLY BE INTERRUPTION OF SUCH BASIC SERVICES AS LAW ENFORCEMENT, TRANSPORTATION, COMMUNICATION, AND POWER.

W hen you look up and see a bird flying overhead, place an order for fried chicken at the local fast-food place, or visit a farm or zoo and watch the birds scratching for feed on the ground, you probably don't feel frightened or threatened. Why should you? Birds have never seemed particularly scary, unless you count the menacing swarms in Alfred Hitchcock's film *The Birds*. Unfortunately, under those colorful and pretty feathers, some birds are harboring a virus that has not only killed their fellow creatures by the millions, but also represents a serious threat to the lives of untold numbers of humans.

This virus is very similar to the one that caused the Spanish flu epidemic of 1918, so people are understandably worried. While the concern is reasonable, it can also get out of hand. The key to knowing how to react to the avian flu and gauge its actual threat is knowledge. Reading reliable and up-to-date information is essential. Learning as much as you can about the realities (and the rumors) surrounding this flu are the best way for you to respond to what may—or may not—be an international problem.

First of all, put very simply, the avian flu is an infectious disease in birds caused by the H5N1 strain of the influenza virus. Birds are often the carriers of such viruses, which reside in their intestines. Ordinarily, these viruses are relatively mild or even harmless to birds. However, H5N1 is different, and lethal. In birds with the virus, death rates are almost 100 percent. Millions and millions of birds have died from either having the virus or being slaughtered because they are suspected of having it. The H5N1 is a powerful virus; it mutates rapidly and steals genes from viruses in other species. It is possible that with the proper pattern of mutation, it can cause severe and often fatal disease in humans.

CURRENT SITUATION: ANIMAL CASES

Since December 2003, avian influenza infections in poultry or wild birds have been reported in the following countries:

Africa
- Burkina Faso
- Cameroon
- Niger
- Nigeria

East Asia and the Pacific
- Cambodia
- China
- Hong Kong
- Indonesia
- Japan
- Laos
- Malaysia
- Mongolia
- Myanmar (Burma)
- Thailand
- Vietnam

South Asia
- Afghanistan

- India
- Kazakhstan
- Pakistan

Near East
- Egypt
- Iraq
- Iran
- Israel
- Jordan

Europe and Eurasia
- Albania
- Austria
- Azerbaijan
- Bosnia and Herzegovina
- Bulgaria
- Croatia
- Czech Republic
- Denmark
- France
- Georgia
- Germany
- Greece
- Hungary
- Italy
- Poland
- Romania
- Russia
- Serbia and Montenegro
- Slovakia
- Sweden
- Switzerland

- Turkey
- Ukraine

THE FIRST APPEARANCE IN HUMANS

The avian flu first grabbed the medical world's attention in 1997. It appeared in Hong Kong, and it was killing poultry in shocking numbers. Farmers knew something was wrong because their birds were not behaving normally. They showed signs of sickness, like quietness, a drop in egg production, swollen or congested combs, swelling of the skin under the eyes, diarrhea, and bleeding. Soon birds begin to die, first only a few, then in increasing numbers.

When avian flu is suspected on a poultry farm, a farmer calls a veterinarian to find out what is wrong. The vet then orders tests to determine if a flu virus is present. If the test comes back positive for avian flu, further tests are conducted to identify the strain of flu that is present in the bird's system. If the strain is an H7 or H5, samples are sent away to identify the subtype.

In May 1997, the flu situation turned from worrisome to terrifying—the first human caught the avian flu and died. Studies showed that the virus could be transmitted through a bird's nasal secretions, saliva, and feces (solid waste). It could be transported from one place to another via clothing, workers' shoes, or tractor wheels. Anyone who killed, defeathered, butchered, or prepared an infected bird was at high risk. Open-air markets where people sell their chickens are considered hotbeds of infection because they are often crowded and unsanitary.

Toward the end of 1997, eighteen more people were diagnosed with avian flu, and six of them died. Millions of chickens and ducks were killed to try and stop the spread of this new disease. Each patient was shown to have been in contact with either the bird's secretions or surfaces where these secretions had been such as cages, water and feed, or equipment. Then, just as organizations like the CDC and WHO began to investigate, the virus seemed to fade away. In essence, it dropped out of sight for six years, only to return at the end of December 2003 in a most unexpected place.

In a Thailand zoo, two tigers and two leopards died after eating fresh, raw chickens that were identified as contaminated with H5N1 virus. It was the first time that bird flu had ever been observed in large felines. This second wave of avian flu hit hard. There were reports of the flu among poultry in South Korea, Cambodia, Indonesia, Japan, Laos, Thailand, and Vietnam. Three human deaths were reported in Vietnam in December.

SYMPTOMS OF AVIAN FLU IN HUMANS

In humans, avian flu symptoms are much like those of any flu, except they are faster and more intense. They often take one to five days after exposure to the virus to begin appearing.

- Fever
- Aches

- Cough
- Eye infections
- Respiratory distress
- Sore throat
- Pneumonia

CURRENT SITUATION: HUMAN CASES

Since January 2004, the WHO has reported human cases of avian influenza A in the following countries:

East Asia and the Pacific
- Cambodia
- China
- Indonesia
- Thailand
- Vietnam

Europe and Eurasia
- Azerbaijan
- Turkey

Near East
- Egypt
- Iraq

AVIAN FLU TAKES ROOT

Throughout 2004, reports of avian flu continued. Flocks in the previously affected countries, as well as China and Malaysia, were dying. Those poultry that did not die from the disease were slaughtered just in case they were harboring it. Poultry fatalities numbered in the millions. Fortunately, the number of human cases grew much slower. Research showed that H5N1 was growing in power and proving ever more dangerous to wild waterfowl and even some mammals. By the end of the year, there had been a total of thirty-two human deaths in Thailand and Vietnam.

In 2005, even more birds succumbed to the flu in a number of countries. In addition, forty-one people died in Thailand, Vietnam, China, Cambodia, and Indonesia. In September of that year, Dr. Nabarro of the United Nations called on many of the world's governments to take immediate steps to confront the potential crisis of avian flu. "That rampant, explosive spread and the dramatic way it's killing poultry so rapidly suggests that we've got a beastly virus in our midst," he said.[1]

The following month, President George W. Bush invited drug manufacturers to a meeting at the White House to encourage them to step up the process of creating a bird flu vaccine. He said, "A pandemic is unlike other natural disasters. Out-breaks can happen simultaneously in hundreds, or even thousands, of locations at the same time. And unlike storms or floods which strike in an instant and then recede, a pandemic can continue spreading destruction in repeated ways that can last for a year or more."[2] The U.S. secretary of Health and Human Services also set up a new service organization called the National Influenza Pandemic Preparedness Task Force.

The first half of 2006 saw a continued progres-sion of the disease. In January, seven more people died in Turkey, Indonesia, and China. Iraq reported its first human death, indicating the disease was spreading beyond Asia. The following month, thirteen new countries reported their first H5N1 infections in wild and domestic birds. According to the WHO, 170 people have contracted the flu, and 92 have died since 2003. In late June 2006, Michael O. Leavitt, secretary of the Department of Health and Human Services, issued "Pandemic Planning Update II." In it, he stated that the H5N1 virus has been confirmed in fifty-three countries. There have been 228 confirmed human cases, with more than 100 deaths. The most troubling fact in the entire report focused on a flu cluster in an Indonesian family, however. When a woman contracted the flu following exposure to infected poultry, she infected six other family members. All died but one. Both the WHO and CDC rushed to the scene to administer antivirals to people in the neighboring area and to perform tests to find out how the virus had spread directly from one person to another—a prerequisite for a pandemic. Tests revealed that the virus had mutated slightly in one of the young victims—the first evidence that this was possible.

HOW MANY HUMANS MIGHT DIE?

As hard as it is to predict whether or not a pandemic is coming, it is even harder to predict what effects it might have if it does arrive. The number of deaths from any pandemic depends on several factors: how many people are infected, how virulent the virus is, how vulnerable a population is, and how effective preventive measures are. The CDC and WHO have estimated that if the avian flu should mutate into a human flu, 20 million to 47 million humans could become sick, with between 2 million and 7.4 million dying worldwide.

Some researchers and epidemiologists believe it would take about ninety days for a full-fledged avian flu pandemic to sweep across the entire planet, while computer models predict it would be closer to twenty-four days. It is also predicted that the cost to the world's economy of a deadly pandemic would range between $71.3 and $166.5 billion. Hospitals would be completely overwhelmed, businesses would go bankrupt due to lost workers and customers, and there would probably be interruption of such basic services as law enforcement, transportation, communication, and power.

HOW CAN IT GET HERE?

Currently, there are three main ways that the avian flu could get to this country. Since the United States has already banned buying birds from any affected countries, it is not likely to sneak in on grocery shelves. Instead, experts believe it will arrive on American shores in one of these ways: migratory birds, exotic and illegal bird sales, and cockfighting.

Migratory Birds

Every autumn, birds fly to regions with warmer climates, and then fly back again with the return of spring. Scientists are worried that these migratory birds will pick up the H5N1 virus before migrating, stay healthy long enough to complete the journey, and then spread it wherever they land before dying of the disease. The spring migration from Asia to Alaska is particularly worrisome, since the flu is so much more prevalent in the Asian regions.

To address this concern, many experts are trying to pinpoint major migratory routes and screen the birds as they enter the country. Although they are currently examining five to six times as many birds as they did just a few years ago, it is still an over-whelming project. In addition, migratory routes cannot always be predicted. They can vary from year to year and can be quite complex. "[Migrating birds can show up] virtually anywhere and come from virtually anywhere," explains Ken Rosenberg, Director of Conservation Science at Cornell Laboratory of Ornithology in New York. "That's just the nature of birds and bird migration."[3]

THE RAVENS OF THE TOWER OF LONDON

In February 2006, the people of London saw something—or didn't see something—for the first time in 300 years: there were no ravens on the grounds of the Tower of London. English legend says that a terrible evil will befall the kingdom if ever the Tower of London loses its ravens. King Charles II (1660–1685) had originally decreed that at least six ravens had to remain at the tower at all times. Ever since then, the birds have been there. Tourists and other visitors even knew them by name: Baldrick, Branwen, Gwyllum, Hugine, Munin, and Thor.

However, as of the beginning of 2006, the ravens have been kept inside the tower because of concerns about them contracting the avian flu. They have been moved inside to an aviary and will stay there until the worry has passed.

Sales of Exotic Birds

A second way that avian flu could reach the United States is through the ongoing problem of exotic—and illegal—bird sales and smuggling. A perfect example is what happened in October 2004 when a man was caught at Brussels International Airport in Belgium smuggling two crested hawk eagles into Europe from Thailand. The live birds had been stuffed into long black tubes and put in his carry-on luggage. Although the man claimed he had brought the birds back as a present for his brother, it was later proven that he was selling them to a Belgian falconer. These eagles were killed and tested positive for H5N1. Immediately, everyone who had been in contact with the birds, as well as the veterinarian who had treated and tested them, was examined and kept in quarantine. Only the veterinarian showed any signs of the virus, and luckily it was a mild case.

Statistics show that 400,000 live exotic birds are imported to the United States each year as pets. At least a quarter of these birds come in illegally. According to the government, the illegal wildlife trade ranks in profitability second only to illegal drug trafficking. Parrots are especially popular because people like their bright colors. There are more than 330 parrot species in the world, and all but two are protected under the convention on International Trade in Endangered Species of Wild Fauna and Flora. Forty-five parrot species on the list are at the highest level of protection, and all commercial trade in them is prohibited. The other protected parrot species cannot be exported without sellers first getting export permits from the birds' country of origin.

U.S. regulations require that all imported wild birds must spend thirty days in government quarantine stations to make sure they are healthy. Obviously, with birds smuggled in secretly and illegally, there is no opportunity for such quarantine and protection. If someone smuggles in birds that have the H5N1 virus, it could quickly spread to other birds in this country. This, in turn, would increase the chance of the virus mutating enough to be able to infect humans. "[E]ach time birds are transported, there are many sites where they're handled—at facilities in different airports, in different countries—prior to quarantine. So everyone who's handling those birds can become infected," explains Dr. Teresa Telecky, former director and present consultant for the Wildlife Trade Program at the Humane Society International. "Viruses in birds are often asymptomatic, and blood tests are the only way to find out which one might be present. It can take days for symptoms to develop. That's why we're so worried about these handlers."[4]

Currently, there is a ban on the importation of birds (living or dead) and bird products (eggs, etc.) into the United States from all affected countries. As of March 29, 2006, the list of banned countries included:

- Afghanistan
- Albania
- Azerbaijan
- Burma
- Cambodia
- Cameroon
- China
- Egypt
- France
- India
- Indonesia
- Israel
- Japan
- Jordan
- Laos
- Kazakhstan
- Malaysia
- Niger
- Nigeria
- Romania
- Russia
- South Korea
- Thailand
- Turkey
- Ukraine
- Vietnam

Cockfighting

The third way that avian flu could spread quickly in this country is through the practice of cockfighting, in which two roosters are placed in a ring and fight each other, usually to the death. People place bets on which rooster will win. Cockfighting is hugely popular throughout Asia, particularly in Thailand and the Philippines. They have millions of fighting cocks (roosters) there. Fights are even televised for fans to watch and gamble on.

Although cockfighting is illegal in forty-eight states, it is still legal in Louisiana and New Mexico. It is performed illegally in many more states across the nation as well. People bet hundreds, even thousands, of dollars on these matches, and it is not uncommon to have more than a million dollars change hands in the aftermath of a fight. Each day, tens of thousands of fighting birds travel across the country. If they happen to be infected, H5N1 goes along for the ride, too.

Since fighting cocks can earn their owners a lot of money, they are often tended carefully and handled intimately. For example, if a gamecock is injured, the handler will often come into direct contact with the very substances that can transmit the avian flu virus.

"There's a lot of hands-on interaction between the handlers and the roosters in all cockfights," says John Goodwin, deputy manager for animal fighting issues at the Humane Society. "When an injured cock is spitting up blood, its handler will put his mouth over the cock's beak to suction out the blood. We've been told that at least several of those killed by bird flu in Thailand were directly involved in cockfighting . . . The problem is, bird flu is still seen as a joke among those in the cock-fighting community in the United States," he continues. "They're not taking the possible risks seriously. Even in Thailand, there's still tremendous ignorance about how the bird flu can be transmitted from infected roosters . . . After the bird flu killed those men, the Thai government enacted a temporary ban on all blood sport. But we know it's being defied all the time."[5]

It is likely that with these three areas of national vulnerability—migration, illegal imports, and cockfighting—bird flu will reach the United States. Experts believe it will happen before the end of 2006. Will the country be ready? No one is quite sure. As Klaus Stohr, project leader for the WHO's Global Influenza Program, said at a news conference in May 2005, "With this virus we have had very many surprises; we have had a very steep learning curve. We are seeing that it is changing very rapidly." He added, "So we do not know if a pandemic can occur next week or next year, or perhaps if another virus is going to cause a pandemic. We should simply continue with our pandemic preparedness."[6]

CHAPTER SIX

Avian Flu Survivor Stories

I WAS SO WEAK I COULD NOT GET UP. I FELT LIKE MY HEART WAS GOING TO STOP BEATING. I FELT SO EXHAUSTED . . . I FELT AS IF I WAS IN HELL.

W ith fewer than 200 people who have actually experienced the avian flu and survived, finding someone who knows what it is like to be infected with it and successfully fight it off is not easy. There are a few fortunate people, however, who have grappled with this disease and lived to tell the tale. Here are the true stories of three of them.

ABLE TO SMILE

Four-year-old Selami Bas's family does not have a lot of possessions. The only piece of furniture in their home in Yakubiye, a poor neighborhood in southeast Turkey, is a simple low cushion. As Selami sits there cross-legged, however, he has a big smile on his face. He is a lucky person; he had avian flu and survived.

In early January 2006, Selami and his father, Mehmet Bas, were visiting Selami's grandfather's house in a village about fifty miles (eighty kilometers) east of the city. While he was there, the young boy developed a cough and temperature. Soon, he also had a stomachache and sore throat. Mehmet Bas, a construction worker, immediately took his son to the state children's hospital.

The hospital staff was already on high alert to watch for any potential avian flu victims, especially children. In the preceding two days, they had lost three children to the illness. When they discovered that Selami had been playing with chickens at his grandfather's house, they promptly administered Tamiflu, a medication that attacks flu viruses. His test results came back two days later: Selami was indeed positive for avian flu. Yet Selami survived, and within two weeks he was released from the hospital, completely recovered.

Why did Selami survive when others his age did not? Some believe it is because his father did not hesitate to take him to the hospital and get him treatment. The early administering of Tamiflu was probably also an important factor in his recovery.[1]

TOO MUCH TORTURE

Many people who have been through the experience of a tornado marvel at how it can completely destroy one house and leave the neighboring house a few feet away untouched. A similar sensation must have struck thirty-five-year-old Pranom Thongchan of Srisomboon, at the edge of Thailand's central plains.

First, she watched as all of her chickens began dying. Next, her eleven-year-old niece, Sakuntala, fell ill. "She came back from school and suddenly she got a high fever," says Pranom. They went to the doctor and he gave the young girl medicine to lower the fever. Sakuntala kept going to school for five more days. On the sixth day, her stomach hurt. "I wasn't worried at the time, but then the symptoms developed into something quite serious," says Pranom. "She could not breathe properly." A hospital X-ray showed that Sakuntala's lungs were in serious trouble. She was immediately transported to another hospital, but died along the way. "By the time she arrived at the hospital, she had no lungs," describes Pranom. "It happened so fast. She was coughing intensely just before she died. Her mother saw her daughter in pain, so she tried to soothe her, held her, hugged and kissed her daughter."[2]

At the funeral three days later, Sakuntala's mother, Pranee Sodchoen, began to feel ill. "It was like a normal fever, normal headache, and dizziness," says Pranom. Three days later, Pranee returned to her home in Nonthaburi, outside Bangkok. "She had a smile on her face and looked like normal," recalls Pranom. Within a couple of days, she was in intensive care, and Pranom was not feeling well either. "I felt a little bit of fever and my body ached," she says.[3]

Two days later, she, too, developed a raging headache that would not go away, no matter what she tried. Despite her illness, Pranom went to the market. When she got back home, things were definitely worse. "That evening when I came back, it was like extreme fever. I felt dizzy and faint. My hands turned pale; it seemed like there was no blood in my body. The next morning, I hardly had the energy to walk. I had to crawl out of bed, and I felt as if my body was shriveling."[4]

At the local hospital, Pranom was given standard flu medication and sent back home. That evening, she began to cough. "I knew inside myself it was getting worse, and that night I heard my sister had died . . . I was worried, but I couldn't speak to anybody because I didn't want to scare them," she says. "I didn't think I was going to die—I tried not to think that way."[5]

The next night, the cough became worse. Specialists from Bangkok—hearing of what had happened to her sister and niece, and fearing they were witnessing the first person-to-person transmission of the bird flu—came to examine her. "They separated everybody from me," recalls Pranom. "I had a fever all the time, feeling cold and shivering and shaking. I couldn't bear it anymore. I said to the doctor, 'Just do whatever you want to do because I feel I am going to die.'"[6] Soon, she found herself in a hospital with needles in her arm and an oxygen mask on her face. Her treatment went on for six days, during which she lay in the hospital bed thinking of her sister and niece. She was waiting for her own death to arrive.

"By that time, I was so weak, I could not get up," she explains. "I felt like my heart was going to stop beating. I felt so exhausted. I did not have the energy to speak or pay attention to anything. I felt as if I had been running for days or years, and I could not breathe. It was so tiring and exhausting. I had no energy left in my body, almost no life. I felt as if I was in hell."[7]

Unlike her niece and sister, however, Pranom suddenly began to recover from her bout of avian flu. On the seventh day, her fever broke. "I felt brand new," she says. "I could take a deep breath for the first time. Three days after that I could stand up, walk a little bit, and put a smile on my face." Pranom soon went home, and a few months later she felt perfectly normal. Her life has changed, however. There is no more poultry at her house. "I don't want to have chickens anymore," she admits. "I don't have a lot, but it is not worth it happening again."[8]

AN UNFORTUNATE WELCOME

It was supposed to be a festive event. Forty-two-year-old Nguyen Thanh Hung was a construction materials salesman. He had just traveled back to his home city of Thai Binh in Vietnam to visit his brothers. They were happy to see each other. "They threw a welcoming dinner where we had our favorite dish, 'tiet canh,' which is made with chopped, congealed raw duck blood and herbs," explains Hung. "The duck was plump and looking healthy, so we didn't have the slightest suspicion that it might be sick. Moreover, we were thinking chicken flu only exists in the south of the country."[9]

One day after the family dinner, Hung's oldest brother, Nguyen Hung Viet, did not feel well. He had a temperature. Rather than head to the doctor, however, the family waited a week to see if he would get better on his own. He didn't. They knew it was time to seek help.

"It was New Year's Day," recalls Hung. "The hospital was running on minimal staffing, and only got back to normal operating schedule three days afterwards. It was unfortunate timing for him. At that point, my brother was already too weak. He couldn't breathe; his left lung was totally damaged. Yet the doctors did not think he had bird flu and his tests came back negative. So, I didn't take any preventive measures while taking care of him. I spent days and nights next to his sick-bed, yet I didn't even bother with a mask."[10]

On January 10, 2005, Nguyen Hung Viet died. Later that day, Hung came down with a fever of his own. "I guess we both got it from the last meal we shared together," he speculates. "I got really worried, so the next day I went to a clinic where they took a scan of my lungs," he says. "The result came back not so good, and when I complained about difficulties in breathing, they referred me to the same hospital where my brother was treated. In a way, I was lucky at that time; a number of people had died in the south of bird flu, and the media was raising the alarm about this matter. I was immediately put into quarantine. My concern grew each day, as my temperature was staying extremely high. At the worst moment, two-thirds of one lung was severely affected," he explains.[11]

Next came the diagnosis—and terror. "[W]hen the doctors told me I had bird flu, I was totally shocked," he admits. "I knew nothing about it, and it scared me. The test on the specimen taken from my brother also came back that day as positive. I got into such a panic, even though my fever was beginning to subside. For two nights, I didn't sleep."[12]

Time passed slowly for Hung. "I told myself I should not doze off at any point," he remembers. "Something may happen inside me, inside my brain, and I may never wake up." To everyone's surprise, however, Hung began to get better. "Only when my fever had gone and the doctors told me my lungs had made a miraculous recovery did I feel a little relieved."[13] He was released days later and returned home to his wife and children. Although he had made a complete recovery, his life was not to be the same.

First, he took a leave of absence from work, much to his employer's relief. "They were only too happy to release me," he says. "Not everybody believes that I don't have the virus anymore and that it is not easy to contract bird flu virus. It is like having a stigma; some people look at you with suspicion and fear. So I think it's best to avoid having too much contact with other people."[14]

Having avian flu also changed Hung's outlook on his family's lifestyle. "I look out for any slightest symptoms of bird flu in my family," he admits. "I'm watching like a hawk. We have also stopped eating chicken, duck, and poultry in general. Maybe it is too cautious, but we cannot risk our health. We have to stay alert, very alert," he adds, and then chuckles. "I now know everything about preventing bird flu. I should be employed by the Health Ministry to do their awareness campaign."[15]

CHAPTER SEVEN

Strategies and Treatments

FEELING HELPLESS IN THE FACE OF A POTENTIAL PANDEMIC MAY BE UNDERSTANDABLE, BUT IT IS ALSO MISTAKEN . . . KEEP INFORMED AND KEEP CALM. INFORMATION AND HELP WILL BE THERE WHEN— OR IF—YOU NEED THEM.

A lthough media reports and talk on the street may make it sound like people are powerless in the battle against an avian flu pandemic, that is just not true. With each passing day, it becomes even less true. Vaccines are being developed, antiviral drugs are being stockpiled, and other avenues of treatment and preparation are being explored.

As of November 2005, President George W. Bush made avian flu treatment a high priority for the entire nation. Working in conjunction with the WHO, the CDC, the Food and Agriculture Organization, the World Organization for Animal Health, and the Asia-Pacific Economic Cooperation Forum, he requested that Congress authorize the spending of $7.1 billion to prepare for the possibility of a pandemic. As he put it, "A pandemic is a lot like a forest fire. If caught early, it might be extinguished with limited damage; if allowed to smolder undetected, it can grow to an inferno that spreads quickly beyond our ability to control it."[1] This plan would provide funding for early detection, containment, and treatment of an avian flu outbreak. It also includes a call for improving the process of manufacturing vaccines and stockpiling antiviral drugs.

The money would be divided into several different projects. Two hundred and fifty-one million dollars would be earmarked to help other countries train medical personnel and increase awareness of potential outbreaks. Just over $1 billion would go toward purchasing enough bird flu vaccine for twenty million people. Although that vaccine has not been perfected yet, whatever still-experimental vaccine exists at the time of the emergence of a pandemic could probably help stem a rising tide of sickness. "A vaccine against the current avian flu virus would likely offer some protection against a pandemic strain and possibly save many lives in the first critical months of an outbreak," explained Bush.[2]

Another $2.8 billion would go to fund a "crash program" to speed up the development of new technology so vaccines could be produced faster. Without this new technology, manufacturers could never make enough vaccine in time should a pandemic actually occur. Right now, vaccines are still made using 1950s technology. "In the event of a pandemic," said President Bush, "this antiquated process would take many, many months to produce a vaccine, and it would not allow us to produce enough vaccine for every American in time."[3] An additional $1 billion would be allotted for stockpiling antiviral drugs and $583 million for general "pandemic preparedness" at local, state, and federal levels.

NATIONAL PANDEMIC INFLUENZA PLAN

1. Pre-Pandemic
   - Reduce opportunities for human infection
   - Strengthen early warning system through surveillance and detection

2. Emergence of Pandemic Virus
   • Contain and delay the spread at the source

3. Pandemic Declared and Spreading Internationally
   • Reduce morbidity and mortality by limiting the spread of the outbreak and mitigating its health and economic impacts and social disruptions
   • Conduct research to guide response measures

A FUTURE VACCINE

There are a number of ways that the nation can protect against the devastation of an avian flu pandemic. Most of these measures—like culling any birds that have been exposed to H5N1 or show symptoms of the flu—have been in place for more than a year. Close surveillance systems have also been set up. Vaccines are being explored and antiviral medications are being stockpiled.

While a vaccine is probably the best way to combat an illness like the avian flu, one simply is not available yet to counteract H5N1. Until the virus passes directly from one person to another, experts will not have access to the genetic materials necessary to make an effective human vaccine. Until then, they can only guess at how the virus may mutate to make person-to-person contact possible, and how those mutations may alter the strength and progression of the illness.

In August 2005, the government agreed to purchase millions of doses of a prototype bird flu vaccine based on a current strain from a French manufacturer. The prototype is to be licensed by the end of 2006, following extensive testing. Once it is passed, it will take another six to twelve months to get it into production. No one is sure how effective it will be. It is a very potent vaccine, more than six times the strength of typical vaccines.

If and when the vaccine is created, developed, produced, and prepared to be administered, the government will distribute it to people in the following order of priority:

Tier 1, Group A
- Approximately 40,000 people essential to the vaccine's manufacture
- Medical workers with direct patient contact
- Members of the military considered essential to ongoing operations and military medicine

Tier 1, Group B
- People with two or more medical conditions that put them at high risk of flu complications
- People with a past history of hospitalization due to flu

Tier 1, Group C
- Pregnant women
- Household contacts of people with weakened immune systems (patients who have organ

transplants, AIDS, etc.) that prevent them
from being vaccinated
- Household contacts of children under six
months of age

Tier 1, Group D
- Emergency response workers critical to pandemic response
- Key government leaders

Tier 2, Group A
- Healthy people ages sixty-five and older
- People ages six months to sixty-four years with a medical condition that puts them at high risk of flu complications
- Healthy children ages six to twenty-three months

Tier 2, Group B
- Emergency responders not critical to pandemic response
- Public safety workers (firefighters, police, 911 dispatchers, correctional facility staff)
- Utility workers essential for maintaining power, water, and sewage systems
- Transportation workers transporting fuel, water, food, and medical supplies
- Transportation workers providing public ground transportation
- Telecommunications and Internet technology workers essential for network operation and maintenance

Tier 3
- Other key government health decisions makers
- Funeral directors and embalmers

Tier 4
- Healthy people ages two to sixty-four years not included in the above categories.[4]

FLU SURVEILLANCE AND QUARANTINES

An international surveillance system currently exists in more than 150 different countries. In the United States, President Bush launched the National Bio-Surveillance Initiative. The people who work in this system have been trained to watch for three distinct things: multiple cases of a single illness, more severe illnesses than usual, and incidents of flu that occur outside the typical winter season. "This initiative will help us rapidly detect, quantify, and respond to outbreaks of disease in humans and animals, and deliver information quickly to state, local, and national and international public health officials," President Bush said in his speech in November 2005. "By creating systems that provide continuous situational awareness, we're more likely to be able to stop, slow, or limit the spread of the pandemic and save American lives."[5]

Containment methods for the virus, should it appear, include quarantining or isolating infected communities, as well as travel restrictions, school and airport closures, limited public gatherings, and curfews. President Bush has mentioned the possibility of using the military to potentially enforce these emergency measures and has been criticized for it. "The best way to deal with a pandemic is to isolate it and keep it isolated in the region in which it begins," he said. "One option is the use of a military that's able to plan and move," he said. "So that's why I put it on the table. I think it's an important debate for Congress to have."[6]

ANTIVIRAL MEDICATIONS

One way flu has been mitigated (made less severe) in the past is through antiviral medications such as amantadine, rimantadine, oseltamivir (Tamiflu), and zanamivir (Relenza). Each one has positive and negative side effects. Although none of these medications can prevent people from getting the flu, they can lessen the symptoms. Amantadine has been on the market since 1976. It interferes with a virus's ability to replicate, or make copies of itself. It has been reported to cause nervousness, anxiety, insomnia, and light-headedness. Rimantadine came on the market in 1993 and works the same way as amantadine. Unfortunately, about 12 percent of people are resistant to this medication.

Both Tamiflu and Relenza were released in 1999 and they work to block the enzyme that the virus needs in order to escape from one cell and infect another. Relenza is an inhaled powder, which makes it hard to administer to people who are already coughing and having trouble breathing. Tamiflu seems to be the most effective of the bunch, and it is the one the government is stockpiling. Currently, the WHO has between three and five million doses of it for use at the first sign of an avian flu outbreak. In addition to stockpiling medication, the government is also gathering emergency-related medical supplies and equipment in a project called Strategic National Stockpile.

NATURAL ANTIVIRALS

If you want to start taking your own daily dose of antivirals, you don't have to wait around for a prescription. There are some natural antivirals that you can get at your local health food store and use on a routine basis:

- Garlic (raw)
- Vitamin C
- Green tea
- Saint-John's-wort
- Apple juice
- Skullcap

These natural substances help fight mild viruses and boost your immune system. They won't protect you against avian flu virus specifically.

But they may increase your general health and strengthen your immune system, possibly making you less vulnerable to infection.

Feeling helpless in the face of a potential pandemic may be understandable, but it is also mistaken. Hundreds of people are putting plans into place, from doctors and nurses at the local clinic to the heads of the federal government. Keep informed and stay calm. Information and help will be there when—or if—you need them.

CHAPTER EIGHT

Staying Safe, Staying Calm

THE GREATEST PROBLEM AMONG
MY PATIENTS RIGHT NOW ISN'T
BIRD FLU; IT IS FEAR OF BIRD FLU.
THE GREATEST RISK OF AN EPI-
DEMIC IS A FEAR EPIDEMIC . . .
FEAR IS INFECTIOUS.

Are you worried about the avian flu now? Do the evening news reports and newspaper and magazine articles make you feel like doom is just around the corner? Do you comb online news sites for information that indicates a pandemic is imminent? If so, you may be making yourself unwell even without coming into contact with the flu virus.

AN EPIDEMIC OF FEAR

Although the dangers of catching avian flu in North America are real, they are also, at this point, purely theoretical. The avian flu may arrive in the United States, and it may not. If it arrives, it may make the leap from birds to humans, or it may not.

Being terribly worried and constantly afraid, however, is a real and immediate danger. It can cause emotional and physical stress, resulting in high blood pressure, chest pain, anxiety, shortness of breath, headache, and even depression. Dr. Marc Siegel writes, "The greatest problem among my patients right now isn't bird flu; it is fear of bird flu. The greatest risk of an epidemic is a fear epidemic . . . Fear is infectious." He continues, "And fear of bird flu has become particularly virulent. There is a vaccine for this fear: it is called information mixed with perspective. Since there is a shortage of this vaccine, fear has begun to spread throughout my community and yours. That is a chilling foretaste of the horror of a true epidemic."[1]

While burying your head in the sand or ignoring what is going on is not the wisest course, neither is obsessing about the possibility of a pandemic. As Anthony Fauci, director of the National Institute of Allergy and Infectious Diseases at the National Institutes of Health puts it, "The one thing I can say is that you often hear that we're one mutation away from having a pandemic that spreads everywhere. Well, yes and no. Let me concentrate on the 'no.' That implies that it's a very simple event to get a virus that is very poorly transmissible to become highly transmissible. No, a lot of different things have to happen to that virus for it to be able to go from very poorly efficient to highly efficient." Fauci adds, "[H]ealth officials like myself have to assume a) that will happen, and b) it will be a worst-case scenario because you have to gear up your preparation. But when the American public gets up in the morning and goes to work, they should not be fixating that we're one mutation away from disaster."[2]

The three typical ways that the public reacts to a disaster like a pandemic are:

1. **Denial:** "There's no way this is really happening. It is just being overhyped by the media."
2. **Hysteria:** "This will be just like Hurricane Katrina. We are doomed. No one will help us."
3. **Optimism, rationality, and pragmatism:** "I need to hope for the best and prepare for the worst!"

The third reaction is the healthiest and most prudent. It is important to balance legitimate cause for concern with equally legitimate reasons for confidence and optimism. A close examination of the many differences that exist between the 1918 Spanish flu disaster and today's threat of avian flu highlights both the areas of greater concern and those that offer reassurance that a large-scale, worldwide catastrophe is unlikely.

ARE AMERICANS WORRIED?

In February 2006, the Harvard School of Public Health conducted the first official telephone survey of Americans to learn how the general public felt about the avian flu threat. Out of the 1,043 people surveyed, here are the results:

- Fifty-seven percent of respondents are concerned about the bird flu.
- Thirty-three percent believe the flu will appear in the United States by the end of 2006.
- Forty-six percent of the people who eat chicken said they would stop eating it if the bird flu hit the U.S. poultry industry.
- Seventy-five percent said they would reduce or avoid travel of any kind if there were human outbreaks of the avian flu.
- Seventy-one percent said they would skip public gatherings in the event of an outbreak of avian flu.
- Sixty-eight percent said they would stay at home and keep their kids at home in the event of an outbreak.

- Sixty-eight percent said they would try to get a prescription for an antiviral drug.
- Two percent said they have already talked to their doctors about getting such a prescription now and holding onto it in case of an epidemic.

REASONS FOR OPTIMISM AND CONFIDENCE

The world has changed dramatically since 1918. The following developments present us with greater challenges to overcome when attempting to stave off or grapple with a global pandemic:

- The world has larger populations living in closer quarters than in 1918. This means a virus has the ability to spread easier and faster.
- Because of the ease of international travel, a pandemic would spread much quicker than it did in 1918, when smaller numbers of people traveled shorter distances, going from place to place by horse, steamship, or train.
- Because of the high-tech communication systems that now exist, it is possible to quickly send and receive helpful information from country to country, but it is equally simple to spread misinformation, rumors, and panic.
- Because of events like the September 11, 2001, terrorist attacks and the catastrophe of Hurricane Katrina, Americans are far closer to the edge of panic than they used to be. Panic can make an already bad situation far worse.

Happily, since 1918, the world has also changed in ways that greatly facilitate attempts to do battle with worldwide pandemics. Consider the following positive factors:

- The Internet allows for the dissemination of immediate, worldwide information and instructions on avoiding crowds, quarantine locations, clinics offering immunization, and other vital facts that will assist in limiting the effects and spread of an epidemic.
- Sanitation procedures and personal hygiene have greatly improved in most parts of the world.
- Doctors are more knowledgeable about the nature of viruses, the properties of disease, the mechanisms of infection and epidemics, and the treatment required to fight specific illnesses.
- Experts have gathered and analyzed important data from previous pandemics and learned valuable lessons as a result.
- Physicians understand viruses better now than at any other time in history.
- Hospitals already have pandemic emergency plans in place. They will be activated the moment signs of a local outbreak become apparent.
- Countries are increasingly aware of the situation, are monitoring their bird and human populations for any signs of sickness, and are sharing information.

- Antiviral drugs exist and are being manufactured and stockpiled for potential use.

The daily news reports, government warnings, and constant Internet chatter about avian flu can make you feel paralyzed by anxiety and uncertainty. One of the best ways to combat this worry is to feel more in control and do something active to address the issue. While there is no medication to take or vaccine to line up for just yet, you can still take some concrete steps to begin fighting avian flu. For example, you can have an emergency plan ready should the pandemic begin and affect your locality. You can ask your physician questions, and discuss your thoughts, fears, and action plan with your parents, teachers, or friends.

BEING PROACTIVE AND PREPARED

The American Red Cross is one of the best resources for learning how to put together an emergency preparedness kit. Here are the basics of what you should keep on hand in order to weather an avian flu pandemic, should one arrive:

- **Water:** You will need water for keeping clean, preparing food, and staying hydrated. How much of it should you have? A good guideline to follow is one gallon of water per day per adult. Don't forget that you will need more if you have pets.

- **Food:** While you can go several weeks without eating (as opposed to only a few days without water), you will be better and more comfortably able to weather any prolonged confinement to your house or restricted opportunities to get fresh provisions if you have some supplies on hand. Experts recommend a three-day supply of nonperishable foods (requiring no refrigeration, cooking, or preparation to eat). Suggestions include canned juices and fruits and vegetables; staples such as sugar, salt, flour, and spices; and high-energy foods such as granola bars and peanut butter. Remember a non-electric can opener, too!

- **First-aid supplies:** It's a good rule to have a first-aid kit on hand for emergencies, like common household cuts, scrapes, splinters, pulled muscles, sprained ankles, etc.—not just something as relatively unlikely as the avian flu. It should include bandages, sterile dressings, gauze pads, antibacterial wet wipes, antibacterial ointment, non-latex gloves, tape, scissors, tweezers, thermometer, aspirin, cough syrup, and face masks. Other things to remember are contact lens supplies, an extra pair of eyeglasses, and a toothbrush and toothpaste.

- **Tools and emergency supplies:** Set aside a storage area in your house—perhaps the basement or pantry—to stow paper cups and plates, plastic utensils, a battery-operated radio, various types of batteries, a flashlight, cash, a tool kit, a fire extinguisher, matches, plastic storage containers, toilet paper, needle and thread, soap, detergent, disinfectant, and bleach for use in an emergency. These supplies will also come in handy in the event of other emergencies, like hurricanes, tornadoes, or snowstorms.

- **Paperwork:** In an emergency—especially if you have to evacuate your house—your family may need quick access to important documents such as wills, insurance policies, deeds, stocks and bonds, medical records and information, passports, Social Security cards, identification cards, tax returns, banking account numbers, credit card account numbers, important phone numbers, and birth, marriage, and death certificates. Have all of these materials stored in a file folder and placed in a location you can easily remember and access.

- **Pets:** Pets will need to be looked after during any emergency. Be sure to store at least several days' worth of the food, water, medication, and plastic bags (for their waste) that they will need. Collect and file their veterinary records.

- **Entertainment:** Time will seem to crawl if you are quarantined or isolated and have not made any provision for distracting yourself. Pack non-electronic forms of entertainment such as books, games, a deck of cards, plenty of paper, and several pens. You probably won't want to waste precious and limited battery power on video games or music.

Remember, it is always wise, in every circumstance, to follow the Boy Scout motto: Be prepared. It is much better to have something on hand and not need it than to need it and not have it.

WHAT ABOUT FACE MASKS?

The good news is that the right face mask can give you an element of protection against the bird flu. The bad news is that most people don't use the correct face mask. The N95 face mask is the most recommended one. It covers both the mouth and nose. Although this type of mask is not necessarily comfortable—especially if you are having trouble breathing or are feverish—it is the most effective. The mask must fit correctly, with a tight seal against the skin, or it will be useless. This mask comes in several different sizes, including a special one for children. Beards and mustaches will prevent a tight seal, so they will have to be shaven off.

TEN GREAT QUESTIONS TO ASK YOUR DOCTOR

1. How likely do you think it is that avian flu will find a way to transmit from person to person?

2. When do you think an avian flu vaccine will be available to the general public?
3. What do you think is the most effective method for treating avian flu in people?
4. Does your office currently have a plan in place for patients should this pandemic occur? Are medications being stockpiled?
5. What precautions should I be taking right now to help lessen the risk of the bird flu?
6. What books have you read, seminars have you attended, or classes have you taken relating to the bird flu?
7. Are there any alternative treatments you can recommend that will help me boost my immune system?
8. How effective do you think President Bush's pandemic plan is?
9. Where do you think our community would quarantine people? Would it be helpful?
10. What plans have you personally made in preparation for a pandemic?

OTHER TIPS FOR STAYING SAFE AND HEALTHY

Keep in mind at all times that at this point, the danger avian flu poses to Americans is minimal. It has not yet been reported here. Even in the most affected countries, the number of infections and deaths is not large. There are many people working hard to develop an effective vaccine. In the unlikely event that you do become infected with the avian flu virus, there are several medications that your doctor can give you.

One of the best things you can do to lessen your risk of getting the bird flu—or any flu, for that matter—is to stay healthy. You can do this by getting enough sleep, eating the healthiest food, and avoiding harmful substances such as tobacco, alcohol, and drugs.

Other suggestions for staying safe include regularly disinfecting the surfaces in your home (like countertops, cutting boards, sinks, and toilets) to lessen the potential germs there. Wash your hands several times a day with soap and consider using an air purifier. Be sure to cough and sneeze into a tissue, and stay at home if you are sick.

Remember that fear is the biggest obstacle to staying healthy. As Dr. Marc Siegel writes, "The fear surrounding avian flu comes not from what is currently happening, but from what-if scenarios."[3] Live your life, enjoy each day to the fullest, prepare for what events seem likely to occur, and don't worry about what you can't control or foresee. You can trust yourself to be able to deal with whatever comes your way, especially if you've already prepared for the most likely occurrences. Until it is time to deal with a problem, enjoy your life, have fun with your family and friends, and stay happy and healthy. You'll be far better prepared to deal with challenges if you have this positive and pragmatic outlook on life.

CHAPTER NINE

Myths and Facts About Avian Flu

IT IS NOT EASY FOR HUMANS TO BECOME INFECTED WITH AVIAN FLU. EVEN PEOPLE WHO HAVE HANDLED INFECTED BIRDS OFTEN DO NOT BECOME INFECTED THEMSELVES.

The idea of a pandemic is scary, and people cope with being scared by talking about what they've heard and read. This means that rumors get started, myths get spread, and facts end up being so misunderstood and distorted that no one is sure what to believe anymore. Here are some of the biggest myths surrounding avian flu. Learn the truth so that when you hear a rumor, you can correct it.

Myth: All types of influenza in birds affect humans.

Fact: Influenza viruses are divided into types A, B, and C. Only type A is truly dangerous. Of the A viruses, it is the subtype H that can mutate into highly pathogenic viruses. Not all influenza-affected birds sicken humans.

Myth: All migratory birds carry avian influenza.

Fact: The role of migratory birds in the spread of avian flu is still unclear. It is true that wild waterfowl are considered to be the natural carriers of all influenza A viruses. They are known to carry the subtypes H5 and H7. However, these are usually in a low pathogenic (mild) form. While some migratory birds may be spreading the H5N1 virus, it is doubtful that all of them are.

Myth: Poultry products can transfer the flu to humans.

Fact: Influenza viruses cannot be passed through properly cooked food. Even if the food was contaminated, the virus cannot survive the heat from the cooking process.

Myth: The entire world is dealing with the avian flu already.

Fact: At this point, the entire world is concerned about the avian flu, but it is only the Asian countries that are truly dealing with its presence. Just over a dozen countries have reported confirmed cases of infected poultry. Of these, only five have confirmed human cases.

Myth: It's easy for humans to become infected with avian flu.

Fact: It is not easy for humans to become infected with avian flu. Even people who have handled infected birds often do not become infected themselves.

Myth: The avian flu is already passing from one person to another.

Fact: This is not true. The people who have contracted the avian flu so far have gotten it from diseased poultry or their waste, saliva, or other bodily secretions. Although there is one suspected case of the flu passing from a child to a mother, it is not confirmed and there have been no other cases since.

Myth: Once human-to-human transmission is achieved, there will be a lethal pandemic.

Fact: This is not truth; it is conjecture. No one knows if the H5N1 virus will ever mutate enough to infect humans in the first place. If it does, there is no way to know what its virulence might be. In fact, if it mutates enough to infect humans, it may mutate into a mild virus instead of a severe one. There is no way of knowing for sure until it happens, if it ever does.

Myth: Some of the best information about the avian flu is on the Internet.

Fact: This could be true, depending on where you do your surfing. Government and public health sites such as the CDC, WHO, and newly created www.pandemicflu.gov, or news sites like CNN or BBC give reliable reports and updates. Unfortunately, there are also a lot of Web sites that are full of sensationalistic rumors, misleading statements, and exaggerated statistics. For instance, companies claim they've created "cures" to the coming bird flu, or e-books declare that for $4.95 you can find the one sure-fire way to prevent ever getting sick. Such wild claims often lead to even wilder fears.

Myth: Current flu vaccines will protect people from the avian flu.

Fact: Modern flu vaccines are designed to provide some protection against seasonal flu strains. However, they have nothing in them that would help anyone stay safe from the bird flu. A vaccine specifically made to counteract the bird flu has not yet been produced, though research and development is well underway.

Myth: Feathers are safe to be touched and handled.

Fact: Because a bird's secretions can get on its feathers, they are actually considered risky to handle. If you do not know where feathers came from, avoid touching them.

Myth: America is not prepared for the avian flu. If it arrives, a chaotic and mismanaged situation could develop, similar to the aftermath of Hurricane Katrina in 2005.

Fact: Katrina unnerved a lot of Americans. They just assumed that in the case of a huge disaster, their government would take care of the situation before it got out of control. The Katrina response was mishandled, and many people lost their homes, possessions, livelihoods, and even their lives as a result. Hopefully, the government will learn from its mistakes and work hard to implement programs, medications, and emergency plans and procedures that will keep the country safe if and when a pandemic should occur.

Myth: The avian flu will be as devastating as the 1918 Spanish flu.

Fact: Fortunately, this is not true. Although there are definite similarities, there are also very important differences that make the avian flu much less of a threat. The medical, informational, technological, and emergency response resources of the twenty-first-century world are vastly superior to those available in 1918.

antigenic A substance that, when introduced into the body, stimulates the production of an antibody.

antiviral Destroying or inhibiting the growth and reproduction of viruses.

asymptomatic Neither causing nor exhibiting symptoms of a disease.

domesticated Describes an animal that has learned how to live in a human environment.

endemic Prevalent in or peculiar to a particular region or people.

epidemic Spreading rapidly and extensively by infection and affecting many individuals in an area or a population at the same time.

epizootic Affecting a large number of animals at the same time within a particular region or area.

inoculate To introduce a serum, vaccine, or antigenic substance into the body of a person or animal, especially to produce or boost immunity to a specific disease.

mutate To change.

outbreak A sudden increase in incidence of a disease.

pandemic Epidemic over a wide area, usually global.

pathogen An agent that causes disease, especially a living microorganism such as a bacterium or fungus.

quarantine A period of time during which a vehicle, person, animal, or material suspected of carrying a contagious disease is detained at a port of entry under enforced isolation to prevent disease from entering a country.

SARS Acronym for sudden acute respiratory syndrome.

stockpile A supply stored for future use, usually carefully gathered and maintained.

surveillance Close observation of a person, group, or situation.

susceptible Likely to be affected; especially sensitive.

vaccine Preparation of a weakened or dead pathogen, like a bacterium or virus, or of a portion of the pathogen's structure, that upon administration stimulates antibody production or cellular immunity against the pathogen, but is incapable of causing severe infection.

virulence Extremely infectious, malignant, or poisonous.

virus Any of the various simple, submicroscopic parasites of plants, animals, and bacteria that often cause disease and that consist essentially of a core of RNA or DNA surrounded by a protein coat. Unable to replicate without a host cell, viruses are typically not considered living organisms.

Centers for Disease Control and
  Prevention
1600 Clifton Road
Atlanta, GA 30333
(800) 311-3435
Web site: http://www.cdc.gov

The Centers for Disease Control and
Prevention (CDC) is at the forefront of public health efforts to prevent and control
infectious and chronic diseases, injuries,
workplace hazards, disabilities, and envi-
ronmental health threats.

National Institute of Allergy and
  Infectious Diseases
National Institutes of Health
Office of Communications and
  Public Liaison
6610 Rockledge Drive, MSC 6612
Bethesda, MD 20892-6612
(301) 496-5717
Web site: http://
  www3.niaid.nih.gov

The National Institute of Allergy and
Infectious Diseases (NIAID) conducts
and supports research to better understand, treat, and ultimately prevent
infectious, immunologic, and allergic diseases. For more than fifty years, NIAID
research has led to new therapies, vaccines,
diagnostic tests, and other technologies
that have improved the health of millions
of people in the United States and around
the world.

U.S. Department of Agriculture
1400 Independence Avenue SW
Washington, DC 20205
Web site: http://www.usda.gov/
  wps/portal/usdahome

The Department of Agriculture provides leadership on food,
agriculture, natural resources, and related issues based on
sound public policy, the best available science, and efficient
management. It seeks to expand markets for agricultural products and support international economic development, further
develop alternative markets for agricultural products and activ-
ities, provide financing needed to help expand job opportunities
and improve housing in rural America, enhance food safety by
taking steps to reduce the prevalence of foodborne hazards
from farm to table, and improve nutrition and health by providing food assistance and nutrition education.

U.S. Department of Health
  Human Services
200 Independence Avenue SW
Washington, DC 20201
(877) 696-6775
Web site: http://www.hhs.gov

The Department of Health and Human Services is the United
States government's principal agency for protecting the health
of all Americans and providing essential human services, especially for those who are least able to help themselves.

U.S. Geological Survey
National Wildlife Health Center
6006 Schroeder Road
Madison, WI 53711-6223
(608) 270-2400
Web site: http://www.nwhc.usgs.gov

The U.S. Geological Survey serves the nation by providing reliable scientific information to describe and understand the earth; minimize loss of life and property from natural disasters; manage water, biological, energy, and mineral resources; and enhance and protect our quality of life.

World Health Organization
Regional Office for the Americas
525 23rd Street NW
Washington, DC 20037
(202) 974-3000
Web site: http://www.who.int/en

The World Health Organization is the United Nations specialized agency for health. Its objective is the attainment by all peoples of the highest possible level of health. Health is defined by the organization as a state of complete physical, mental, and social well-being and not merely the absence of disease or infirmity.

WEB SITES

Due to the changing nature of Internet links, Rosen Publishing has developed an online list of Web sites related to the subject of this book. This site is updated regularly. Please use this link to access the list:

http://www.rosenlinks.com/ccw/avflu

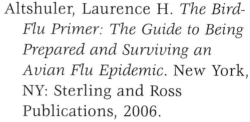

Altshuler, Laurence H. *The Bird-Flu Primer: The Guide to Being Prepared and Surviving an Avian Flu Epidemic*. New York, NY: Sterling and Ross Publications, 2006.

Barry, John M. *The Great Influenza: The Epic Story of the Deadliest Plague in History*. New York, NY: Viking, 2004.

Boire, Martin C. *How to Survive the Bird Flu*. Self-published: MemoMania, LLC, 2005.

Crosby, Alfred W. *America's Forgotten Pandemic: The Influenza of 1918*. New York, NY: Cambridge University Press, 2003.

Davis, Mike. *The Monster at Our Door: The Global Threat of Avian Flu*. New York, NY: New Press, 2005.

Layton, Peggy. *Emergency Food Storage and Survival Handbook: Everything You Need to Know to Keep Your Family Safe in a Crisis*. New York, NY: Three Rivers Press, 2002.

Sfakinos, Jeffrey N. *Avian Flu*. New York, NY: Chelsea House Publications, 2006.

Siegel, Marc, M.D. *Bird Flu: Everything You Need to Know About the Next Pandemic*. Hoboken, NJ: John Wiley and Sons, 2006.

Silverstein, Alan. *The Flu and Pneumonia Update*. Berkeley Heights, NJ: Enslow Publishers, 2006.

Woodson, Grattan, M.D. *The Bird Flu Preparedness Planner*. Deerfield Beach, FL: HCI, 2005.

"Avian Influenza (Bird Flu)." Centers for Disease Control. 2006. Retrieved March 2006 (http://www.cdc.gov/flu/avian/).

"Avian Influenza." World Health Organization. 2006. Retrieved March 2006 (http://www.who.int/csr/disease/avian_influenza/en/).

Berger, Sebastien. "Do What You Want—I Feel I Am Going to Die." *Sydney Morning Herald.* October 24, 2005. Retrieved March 2006 (http://www.smh.com.au/news/world/do-what-you-want--i-feel-i-am-going-to-die/2005/10/23/1130006003666.html#).

"Bird Flu (Avian Influenza)." CNN.com. October 2005. Retrieved March 2006 (http://www.cnn.com/HEALTH/library/DS/00566.html).

"Bird Flu: Things to Know, Not Fear." *USA Today.* April 12, 2006. Retrieved April 2006 (http://www.usatoday.com/news/opinion/editorials/2006-04-11-bird-flu_x.htm).

Boire, Martin C. *How to Survive the Bird Flu.* Self-published: MemoMania, LLC, 2005.

"Bush Military Bird Flu Role Slammed." CNN.com. October 6, 2005. Retrieved March 2006 (http://edition.cnn.com/2005/POLITICS/10/05/bush.reax/).

"Bush Unveils $7.1 Billion Plan to Prepare for Flu Pandemic." CNN.com. November 2, 2005. Retrieved March 2006 (http://www.cnn.com/2005/HEALTH/conditions/11/01/us.flu.plan).

Centers for Disease Control. "Key Facts About Avian Influenza (Bird Flu) and Avian Influenza A (H5N1) Virus." Department of Health and Human Services. October 17, 2005. Retrieved June 2006 (http://www.cdc.gov/flu/avian/gen-info/facts.htm).

"Cockfighting Fact Sheet." The Humane Society of the United States. 2006. Retrieved March 2006 (http://www.hsus.org/hsus_field/animal_fighting_the_final_round/cockfighting_fact_sheet).

Davis, Mike. *The Monster at Our Door: The Global Threat of Avian Flu*. New York, NY: The New Press, 2005.

DeNoon, Daniel. "Bird Flu: 10 Questions, 10 Answers." WebMD. January 25, 2006. Retrieved March 2006 (http://www.webmd.com/content/article/113/110741.htm).

Grady, Denise, and Gina Kolata. "How Serious Is the Risk of Avian Flu?" *New York Times*. March 27, 2006. Retrieved April 2006 (http://www.nytimes.com/2006/03/27/health/28qna.html?ex=1144641600&en=eb5c781e30fb6f05&ei=5070).

Greene, Jeffrey, and Karen Moline. *The Bird Flu Pandemic: Can It Happen? Will It Happen?* New York, NY: Thomas Dunne Books, 2006.

Hamilton, John. "Bird Flu Deaths in Thailand Raise Pandemic Fears." NPR.org. December 8, 2004. Retrieved March 2006 (http://www.npr.org/templates/story/story.php?storyId=4209302).

Handwerk, Brian. "Bird Flu: Frequently Asked Questions." *National Geographic News.* March 22, 2006. Retrieved March 2006 (http://news.nationalgeographic.com/news/2006/03/0322_060322_bird_flu.html).

"History of Pandemic Influenza." Aetiology. October 2005. Retrieved March 2006 (http://aetiology.blogspot.com/2005/10/pandemic-influenza-awareness-week-day.html).

"Influenza 1918." PBS.org. 1998. Retrieved March 2006 (http://www.pbs.org/wgbh/amex/influenza).

Kennedy, Bernard. "Turkey: The Smile of a Bird Flu Survivor." UNICEF. Retrieved March 2006 (http://www.unicef.org/ceecis/reallives_3858.html).

Lovett, Richard A. "Bird Flu Will Reach U.S. and Canada This Fall, Experts Predict." *National Geographic News.* March 14, 2006. Retrieved March 2006 (http://news.nationalgeographic.com/news/2006/03/0314_060314_bird_flu.html).

McCurry, Justin. "Bird Flu Suicides in Japan." *Guardian Unlimited.* March 9, 2004. Retrieved April 2006 (http://www.guardian.co.uk/birdflu/story/0,14207,1165302,00.html).

McNeil Jr., Donald G. "Avian Flu: The Worrier; at the U.N.: This Virus Has an Expert 'Quite Scared.'" *New York Times*, March 28, 2006.

Pham, Nga. "Eyewitness: Surviving Bird Flu." *BBC News*. February 1, 2005. Retrieved March 2006 (http://news.bbc.co.uk/go/pr/fr/-/1/hi/world/asia-pacific/4226459.stm).

"President Outlines Pandemic Influenza Preparations and Response." WhiteHouse.gov. November 2005. Retrieved March 2006 (www.whitehouse.gov/news/releases/2005/11/20051101-1.html).

Roach, John. "U.S. Not Ready for Fast-Spreading Flu, Study Finds." *National Geographic News*. April 3, 2006. Retrieved April 2006 (http://news.nationalgeographic.com/news/2006/04/0403_060403_bird_flu.html).

Siegel, Marc, M.D. *Bird Flu: Everything You Need to Know About the Next Pandemic*. Hoboken, NJ: John Wiley and Sons, 2006.

"U.S. Stepping Up Efforts to Fight Bird Flu." Associated Press. March 9, 2006. Retrieved March 2006 (http://www.msnbc.msn.com/id/11741441/).

Van Borm, Steven, et al. "Highly Pathogenic H5N1 Influenza Virus in Smuggled Thai Eagles, Belgium." CDC. July 2005. Retrieved March 2006 (http://www.cdc.gov/ncidod/EID/vol11no05/05-0211.htm).

Chapter 2

1. Marc Siegel, M.D., *Bird Flu: Everything You Need to Know About the Next Pandemic* (Hoboken, NJ: John Wiley and Sons, 2006), p. 59.
2. PBS.org, "Influenza 1918." Retrieved March 2006 (http://www.pbs.org/wgbh/amex/influenza).
3. Ibid.
4. Jeffrey Greene and Karen Moline, *The Bird Flu Pandemic: Can It Happen? Will It Happen?* (New York, NY: Thomas Dunne Books, 2006), pp. 20–21.

Chapter 3

1. Aetiology, "History of Pandemic Influenza." October 2005. Retrieved March 2006 (http://aetiology.blogspot.com/2005/10/pandemic-influenza-awareness-week-day.html).
2. Marc Siegel, M.D., *Bird Flu: Everything You Need to Know About the Next Pandemic* (Hoboken, NJ: John Wiley and Sons, 2006), p. 67.

3. Jeffrey Greene and Karen Moline, *The Bird Flu Pandemic: Can It Happen? Will It Happen?* (New York, NY: Thomas Dunne Books, 2006), p. 97.

Chapter 4

1. Jeffrey Greene and Karen Moline, *The Bird Flu Pandemic: Can It Happen? Will It Happen?* (New York, NY: Thomas Dunne Books, 2006), p. 51.
2. Martin C. Boire, *How to Survive the Bird Flu* (Self-published: MemoMania, LLC, 2005), p. 27.
3. Donald G. McNeil Jr., "Avian Flu: The Worrier; at the U.N.: This Virus Has an Expert 'Quite Scared.'" *New York Times*, March 28, 2006.

Chapter 5

1. Donald G. McNeil Jr., "Avian Flu: The Worrier; at the U.N.: This Virus Has an Expert 'Quite Scared.'" *New York Times*, March 28, 2006.
2. Jeffrey Greene and Karen Moline, *The Bird Flu Pandemic: Can It Happen? Will It Happen?* (New York, NY: Thomas Dunne Books, 2006), p. 12.
3. Associated Press, "U.S. Stepping Up Efforts to Fight Bird Flu." March 9, 2006. Retrieved March 2006 (http://www.msnbc.msn.com/id/11741441/).
4. Jeffrey Greene and Karen Moline, *The Bird Flu Pandemic: Can It Happen? Will It Happen?* (New York, NY: Thomas Dunne Books, 2006), p. 73.
5. Ibid., pp. 75–76.

6. Daniel DeNoon, WebMD, "Bird Flu: 10 Questions, 10 Answers." January 25, 2006. Retrieved March 2006 (http://www.webmd.com/content/article/113/110741.htm).

Chapter 6

1. Bernard Kennedy, UNICEF, "Turkey: The Smile of a Bird Flu Survivor." Retrieved March 2006 (http://www.unicef.org/ceecis/reallives_3858.html).
2. Sebastien Berger, *Sydney Morning Herald*, "Do What You Want—I Feel I Am Going to Die." October 24, 2005. Retrieved March 2006 (http://www.smh.com.au/news/world/do-what-you-want--i-feel-i-am-going-to-die/2005/10/23/1130006003666.html#).
3. Ibid.
4. Ibid.
5. Ibid.
6. Ibid.
7. Ibid.
8. Ibid.
9. Nga Pham, *BBC News*, "Eyewitness: Surviving Bird Flu." February 1, 2005. Retrieved March 2006 (http://news.bbc.co.uk/go/pr/fr/-/1/hi/world/asia-pacific/4226459.stm).
10. Ibid.
11. Ibid.
12. Ibid.

13. Ibid.
14. Ibid.
15. Ibid.

Chapter 7

1. CNN.com, "Bush Unveils $7.1 Billion Plan to Prepare for Flu Pandemic." November 2, 2005. Retrieved March 2006 (http://www.cnn.com/2005/HEALTH/conditions/11/01/us.flu.plan).
2. Ibid.
3. WhiteHouse.gov, "President Outlines Pandemic Influenza Preparations and Response." November 2005. Retrieved March 2006 (http://www.whitehouse.gov/news/releases/2005/11/20051101-1.html).
4. Daniel DeNoon, WebMD, "Bird Flu: 10 Questions, 10 Answers." January 25, 2006. Rctricved March 2006 (http://www.webmd.com/content/article/113/110741.htm).
5. WhiteHouse.gov, "President Outlines Pandemic Influenza Preparations and Response."
6. CNN.com. "Bush Military Bird Flu Role Slammed." October 6, 2005. Retrieved March 2006 (http://edition.cnn.com/2005/POLITICS/10/05/bush.reax/).

Chapter 8

1. Marc Siegel, M.D., *Bird Flu: Everything You Need to Know About the Next Pandemic*

(Hoboken, NJ: John Wiley and Sons, 2006), pp. 178 and 182.

2. *USA Today*, "Bird Flu: Things to Know, Not Fear." April 12, 2006. Retrieved April 2006 (http://www.usatoday.com/news/opinion/editorials/2006-04-11-bird-flu_x.htm).

3. Marc Siegel, M.D., *Bird Flu: Everything You Need to Know About the Next Pandemic*.

A

M

migration, bird, 50, 55, 87
mutation, virus, 6, 18, 36, 37, 42, 51, 67, 76, 89

N

National Bio-Surveillance Initiative, 70
National Influenza Immunization Program, 26
National Influenza Pandemic Preparedness Task Force, 47
National Institutes of Health (NIH), 76

P

pandemics
conditions required for, 37–38
national plan for, 66–67
stages of, 38–39
throughout history, 23–33
pathogen, 39, 87
pneumonia, 19, 31, 46

Q

quarantine, 32, 52, 62, 70, 79, 82

R

Relenza, 71, 72

S

Salk, Jonas, 25

Siegel, Dr. Marc, 27, 75, 85
smallpox, 12, 23, 28
Spanish flu of 1918
countries affected by, 11, 14, 16, 17
death from, 6, 11, 12–13, 14, 17, 19–20, 28
media reportage of, 11, 17
median age of most victims, 17
nicknames for, 9, 11–12, 14, 17, 18, 37
public response to, 14, 15–17
second wave of, 14–16
spread of, 9, 10–11, 14
symptoms of, 11, 12–13, 15, 19
teaching about, 17
theories about, 15
treatment for, 13, 16
Strategic National Stockpile, 72
sudden acute respiratory syndrome (SARS), 29, 31–33
swine flu, 25–27, 29

T

Tamiflu, 58, 71, 72
typhoid, 23, 28

U

United Nations (UN), 39, 47

ABOUT THE AUTHOR

Tamra Orr is a writer living in the Pacific Northwest, which could be one of the important gateways to avian flu should the disease hit American shores. Orr has authored more than thirty nonfiction books for children and families, as well as countless magazine articles, many of them concerning science, medicine, and disease.

Photo Credits: Cover, p. 1 © www.istockphoto.com

Designer: Nelson Sà